Ellie and the Magic Computer

by Jeanette Beaumont

illustrated by Janine Dawson

The Characters

Ellie
is confused about magic.

Gary
likes computer games.

Shashi
has his own
pocket computer.

Mr Bates
takes the computer class.

The Setting

CONTENTS

Chapter 1

Chapter 2

Magic and Computers

Ellie knew about magic. She read stories about magic. In stories things happened and no-one could explain why.

Gary never thought about magic, but he didn't read much. He was Ellie's brother and two years older.

Gary liked computers. When Ellie asked him, "Are computers magic?" Gary laughed.

"Computers only do what they are programmed to do," said Gary.

"What does 'programmed' mean?" Ellie asked.

Gary tried to explain. "A computer is built by people to work out things. People write programs and the computer does what the program says. Shashi and I are going to write some programs soon."

Gary and Shashi had met at computer class. Shashi had his own pocket computer.

Ellie was just about to start going to the class too. The worst part of the class was that it was held in the holidays.

Everyone said how lucky they were to learn how to use the Internet and to play computer games.

But Ellie wasn't any good at computer games. She didn't really like them.

Ellie knew her father wanted her to be good with computers.

"You will be able to find out about everything," he said. "It's magic what computers can do."

Ellie was confused about magic.

CHAPTER 2

Searching the Internet

Their teacher, Mr Bates, was quite old. He wore glasses to see the screen. He had a nice voice.

When he told the class to search the Internet, his mouth made a clicking noise. It was like the sound the computer mouse made!

"Look Ellie," called Gary, "look what Shashi has found on the Internet. A site all about elephants."

Gary knew Ellie liked elephants a lot.
Ellie wouldn't look. She wanted to
find things on her own.

Mr Bates saw Ellie's sad face.

"Use this computer over here, Ellie," he said.

Mr Bates pointed to a strange object in the corner of the room. It did not look like a computer. It looked more like a football.

"I'll leave you to it, Ellie," said Mr Bates.
Then he was gone.

"Where would you like to go today?"
called a voice from the strange-looking
computer. Ellie was startled.

"What do you mean?" she cried.

CHAPTER 3

Who Is This Computer?

"Make up your mind. Make up your mind. What's so hard to decide?" grumbled the voice from the computer.

Ellie felt this was unfair. "I don't know what you mean. I don't know what you are, and I don't know where you came from."

"I'm the brainiest brain," said the voice from the computer. "I mean what I want to mean. I am what I want to be. I go wherever I want to go."

"So you think you know everything," said Ellie.

"Yes", agreed the voice. "WHERE DO YOU WANT TO GO TODAY?"

"I want to ride an elephant," said
Ellie firmly.

"Alone or with them?" asked the
voice, making it clear that he meant
Gary and Shashi.

"With them of course." She liked having friends with her.

Before she could blink, Ellie was
high up on the back of an elephant
with Gary, Shashi and Mr Bates.

Mr Bates had a large hat on his head.

"My grandfather's pith helmet," he
said grandly. "This will come in handy."

CHAPTER 4

The Magic Ride

Mr Bates was right about the need for a hat. The sun was very hot and the elephant walked slowly. Ambled would be the word.

They were at the head of a long chain
of elephants. Each one had a saddle
with wide seats on its back. Shashi
said the saddle was called a howdah.

The elephants seemed to know where
they were going. They made their way
up a steep slope.

Shashi was born in India and knew about elephants. Shashi moved up onto the elephant's head. "Look at the top of the hill," he called.

"Don't shout in my ear," grumbled the elephant. Gary and Shashi were startled.

"Sorry," they both said.

"Hey, this must be India," added Gary.

"Of course it is," said Shashi, "and this is an Indian elephant. You can tell by his ears."

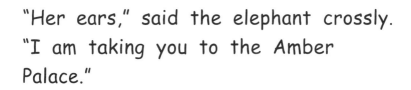

"Her ears," said the elephant crossly.
"I am taking you to the Amber
Palace."

When they reached the top of the hill, there it was. The Amber Palace was grander than anything Ellie had seen in books.

"Ambling to Amber, seated on a howdah," muttered Mr Bates.

The elephants moved faster now.
They seemed to be happy to leave
the dusty road. They walked around
the palace courtyard.

Ellie thought that the people who lived here must have been very splendid.

"Yes indeed, very splendid," said Mr Bates. "What a life they had!"

"Ah yes," agreed the elephant, and she told them all about the time that the prince had ridden on her back.

"It was a very special day. I had bells around my feet. My back was covered with silver and gold."

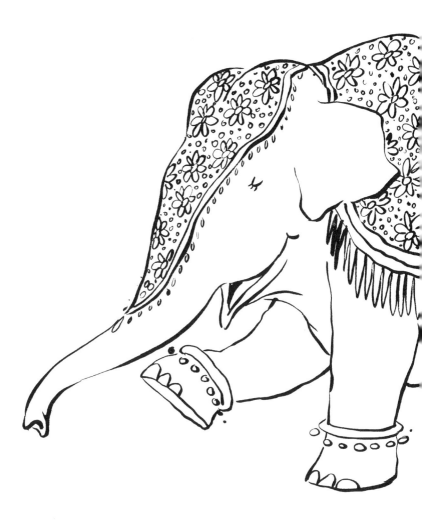

They stopped at a balcony. From here the prince could walk straight onto the back of a standing elephant.

A man stepped onto the balcony. He put something into Ellie's hand. It was a photo of them all on the elephant's back. Ellie put the photo into her pocket.

CHAPTER 5

Ellie Knows What Magic Is

The voice from Ellie's computer called, "You are out of time. Quite out of time!"

The elephant had just walked into a garden. Instead of trees, the garden had huge, stone pillars.

Suddenly, the stone garden became
the playground outside their classroom.
The elephant was gone.

Ellie was with Gary. The class was over. They were waiting to be picked up by their father.

"Hi kids," said their father as he pulled up in the car. "How did you get on today?"

"We rode an elephant," said Ellie. "You are right, Dad. Computers are magic."

Gary laughed. "We were on the
Internet, Dad," he said.

Ellie felt confused again. Had she just imagined the whole thing? Her eyes went all watery.

If she closed her eyes she could still feel the elephant move and sway. She could feel the heat of the sun.

She reached into her pocket for a tissue. She still had the photo!

There they all were on an elephant.
Mr Bates in his pith helmet, Gary and
Ellie on the howdah. Shashi was at
the front on the elephant's head.

"Look Gary," she said, showing him the photo.

"COOL," said Gary. "You made this!
Is that what Mr Bates taught you?
Wait till Shashi sees this. COOL!"

Ellie did not say any more. She knew there were some things you couldn't explain. She held the photo to her chest. She knew about magic.

GLOSSARY

amble
walk slowly

balcony
an outside area up high

explain
to make something clear

confused
mixed up, unsure

howdah
an Indian word for a seat
on an elephant

pillars
tall stone posts

pith helmet
a hard hat worn in
very hot places

site
a place to go
on the Internet

sway
rock from side to side

worst
as bad as it can be

Jeanette Beaumont

What is your favourite breakfast?

Paw paw. (papaya)

Who is your favourite cartoon character?

Bugs Bunny.

What was your least favourite activity at school?

Sewing.

Why is the sky blue?

To match the sea.

Janine Dawson

What is your favourite breakfast?

Fish, rice and soup.

Who is your favourite cartoon character?

Krazy Kat.

What was your least favourite activity at school?

Folk dancing.

Why is the sky blue?

Because it's soothing and refreshing and goes with all the colours the world has to offer. (Have you noticed that it doesn't clash with anything?) So tasteful.